D0021421

NINJAGO
Masters of Spinjitzu

LEGENDS OF SPINJITZU
READER COLLECTION

ADAPTED BY TRACEY WEST

SCHOLASTIC INC.

LEGO® Ninjago: Masters of Spinjitzu (978-0-545-40114-2) © 2011 The LEGO Group.
LEGO® Ninjago: The Golden Weapons (978-0-545-40115-9) © 2011 The LEGO Group.
LEGO® Ninjago: Rise of the Snakes (978-0-545-43592-5) © 2012 The LEGO Group.
LEGO® Ninjago: A Ninja's Path (978-0-545-43593-2) © 2012 The LEGO Group.
LEGO® Ninjago: Pirates vs. Ninja (978-0-545-60800-8) © 2013 The LEGO Group.
LEGO® Ninjago: The Green Ninja (978-0-545-60798-8) © 2013 The LEGO Group.

ISBN 978-0-545-72424-1

10 9 8 7 6 5 4 3 2 1   14 15 16 17 18/0
Printed in China   38

This edition first printing, March 2014

Scholastic Inc.

MIX
Paper from
responsible sources
FSC
www.fsc.org   FSC™ C020056

TABLE OF CONTENTS

MEET THE TEAM

As the sun rose over Ninjago, four young ninja pulled a wagon up a tall mountain. They were on a quest to find the Scythe of Quakes, one of the Four Weapons of Spinjitzu.

In the wagon sat Sensei Wu, their teacher.

Kai, the ninja in red, was the newest member of the team.

"So, where did Sensei find you three?" Kai asked the others.

"I was testing my limits," answered Cole, the ninja in black. "I climbed the tallest mountain without any tools. But when I reached the top, Sensei Wu was there, drinking his tea."

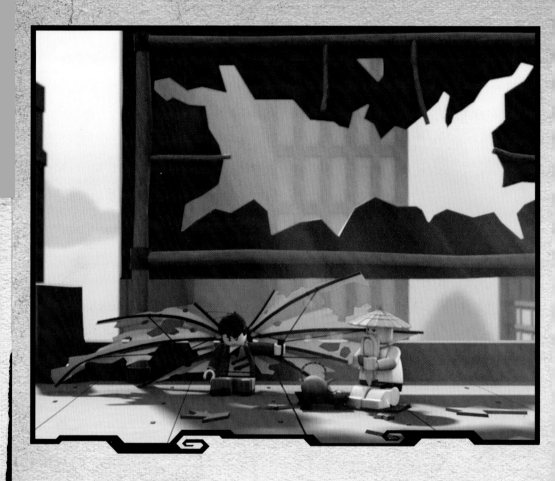

"I was testing my invention," said Jay, the ninja in blue.

Jay had made a pair of wings. He tried to fly . . . only to crash and find Sensei Wu there. He was waiting on a nearby rooftop, drinking his tea.

"And I was testing myself," said Zane, the quiet ninja in white.

Zane was meditating at the bottom of a frozen lake. And somehow . . . Sensei Wu was there underwater, drinking his tea!

THE PLAN

"Stop!" Sensei Wu cried suddenly.

The ninja came to a halt. A large canyon stretched out in front of them. Skeleton warriors were digging into the side of the mountain.

"The Caves of Despair," Sensei said. "Samukai must be close to unearthing the Scythe of Quakes."

"Remember, do not use the Weapon," Sensei Wu warned. "For its power —"

"Yeah, yeah, yeah!" Jay said. He had heard this from Sensei before. "Its power is too much for us mortals." He turned to his friends. "All right guys, let's chop-socky this lemonade stand! Cole, you got the plan?"

"Sure do," Cole replied. "First, we — hey, where's Kai?"

Kai hadn't waited to hear the plan. The ninja saw him sneaking past the skeleton warriors in the canyon.

"Let's go!" Jay cried.

STEALTH ATTACK

Jay, Cole, and Zane jumped into the canyon. They saw rocks coming out of the caves on a conveyor belt. The skeleton warriors checked each rock, looking for the Scythe of Quakes.

One of the warriors spotted Kai! But before he could cry out, the other ninja jumped him.

Bam! Pow! Crunch! Cole, Jay, and Zane made sure the warrior couldn't sound the alarm.

Kai hid behind some big rocks. He looked up at a tall tower in the middle of the canyon. Inside he saw Samukai, King of the Underworld!

"The map!" Kai cried. The map showed where the Four Weapons of Spinjitzu were hidden. Samukai had stolen it from Kai's blacksmith shop.

Nearby, two skeleton commanders were checking rocks on the conveyor belt. Cole, Jay, and Zane slid right under them!

But Kruncha and Nuckal didn't notice.

"I found something!" Nuckal cried, holding up a rock.

"That's another rock, you bonehead!" Kruncha yelled.

"But it's shaped like a donut," Nuckal said. "I wonder if it tastes like one?"

Crunch! Nuckal bit down hard into the rock. *"Ow!"*

Kai climbed to the top of the tall tower. Cole, Jay, and Zane joined him.

Jay smacked Kai on the head. "What's the matter with you?"

"*Shhh!*" Kai warned. He nodded toward a hole in the tower roof. Inside the tower, Samukai was reading the map.

"It's upside down!" Jay realized. "They're digging in the wrong spot!"

THE SCYTHE OF QUAKES

"The Golden Weapon is near," Zane realized. He tied a shuriken to a rope and tossed it down the hole. Samukai didn't see it. The shuriken grabbed the map, and Zane pulled it up through the hole.

"There's no time to waste," Kai said. He did a backflip off the tower and ran off.

"What is it with that guy?" Jay asked. "Always in a rush!"

The ninja raced after Kai toward the spot where the Scythe of Quakes was hidden. A big rock blocked the entrance. Cole, Jay, Kai, and Zane worked together to push it aside.

The Scythe of Quakes lit up the dark cave. The Weapon lay on top of a statue of a dragon's head.

"That is so cool!" Jay cried. His voice echoed through the cave.

"*Shh!* Not so loud!" Cole warned. He jumped on top of the statue, grabbed the Weapon, and tossed it to Kai. "Now let's sneak out while those boneheads are still busy," he said.

Behind them, the statue's mouth slowly began to open. . . .

AN ESCAPE GONE WRONG

The ninja walked outside of the cave . . . right into Samukai and his warriors!

Samukai opened all four of his arms wide. Each bony hand held a sharp dagger. The ninja drew their swords and charged ahead with a battle cry.

"Hii-yaah!"

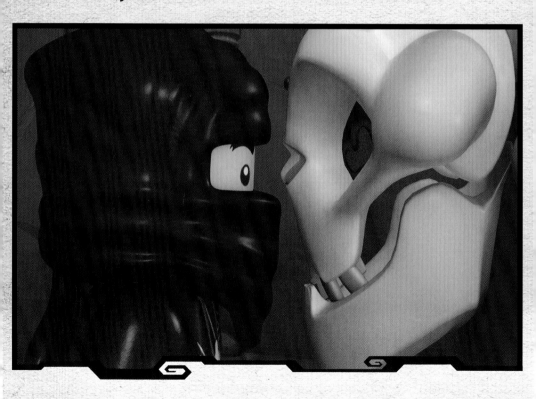

Cole, Jay, Kai, and Zane fought their way through the army of skeleton warriors.

"There's too many of them!" Kai yelled, whacking a skeleton with his sword.

"Let me handle it!" Jay called out. He jumped into the middle of a gang of warriors.

Suddenly, Jay stopped. He looked at the warriors in front of him. Some held long staffs. Others were spinning weapons above their heads.

"Guys, it's just like Sensei's training course!" he realized.

All four ninja had practiced on the course. They wanted to learn Spinjitzu. But so far, none of them could spin like Sensei Wu.

"Over the planks!" Jay cried, jumping from warrior to warrior, knocking them down.

"Dodge the swords!" Jay somersaulted over the heads of the sword-waving warriors.

"Here comes the dummy!" he finished, spinning into another warrior.

MASTERS OF SPINJITZU

Jay kept spinning faster . . . and faster . . . and faster . . . until he became a glowing blue tornado.

"Spinjitzu!" Cole cried.

"Jay, what's the key?" Kai called out.

"I'm just going through the motions!" Jay yelled back.

Kai remembered the training. He jumped. He somersaulted. He spun . . . and he became a spinning tornado!

Cole and Zane got it, too. Soon all four ninja were using Spinjitzu, taking out skeletons left and right.

ENTER THE DRAGON

"Retreat!" Samukai shouted.

The four ninja chased Samukai and his army out of the cave.

Cole flexed his muscles. "Guess they didn't want any more of these babies," he bragged.

Then they all heard a strange, growling noise behind them.

"Um, didn't Sensei say there was a guardian protecting the Weapon?" Zane asked.

The dragon statue wasn't a statue at all — it was a real dragon! The huge beast slowly rose to its feet.

"Is th-th-that what I think it is?" Cole asked nervously.

"I sense we will not be able to spin our way out of this," Zane remarked.

The dragon reared back, opened its mouth, and blasted the ninja with a blazing orange flame.

"*Aaaaaaaaaaaah!*" The ninja screamed as the blast knocked them down.

Cole, Jay, Kai, and Zane raced away as hot dragon fire licked at their heels.

Kai got a gleam in his eye. He removed the cloth that covered the Scythe of Quakes.

"Bad idea, Kai!" Jay warned. "Sensei told us not to use it."

But Kai didn't listen. He ran up to the dragon.

Bam! Kai swung the Scythe and brought it down on the cave floor. The ground began to tremble and crack. The dragon lost its balance and fell.

"We've got to escape!" Cole yelled.

TEAMWORK

The four ninja raced away. But the dragon wasn't down for long. It started to chase them.

"We can use Spinjitzu!" Cole cried. He started to spin, and his friends did the same.

Soon four glowing tornadoes were swirling up the cave walls, heading for an opening in the ceiling.

Cole, Jay, Kai, and Zane escaped through the hole before the dragon could catch them.

"That was so awesome!" Cole cheered. He gave Kai a high-five.

"Yes! We are unbelievable!" Kai yelled.

"We are the best," Zane said proudly.

"Did you see that?" Jay asked. "I was like, *pow! Bam!*"

Sensei Wu joined the four ninja. "Kai, you are part of a team now. Do not forget that." Sensei turned around. "Come! There are three Weapons left."

The four ninja followed Sensei Wu out of the canyon. Now that they had mastered Spinjitzu, they were ready for their next adventure.

LEGO NINJAGO
Masters of Spinjitzu

THE GOLDEN WEAPONS

THE SWORD OF FIRE

"Hooray! We kicked their bony backsides!" Jay said.

Jay, Cole, Kai, and Zane were celebrating. They had defeated the skeleton warriors three times. Now they had three of the Weapons of Spinjitzu. They just needed one more.

Even Sensei Wu was in a good mood. He got up and danced.

Later, while everyone slept, a voice woke Kai. It was his sister, Nya! But how? Samukai had captured her and taken her to Garmadon in the Underworld.

"I have to go," Nya said. She ran off.

Kai raced after her. He followed her to a red temple.

Inside the temple, Kai saw the fourth Weapon of Spinjitzu: the Sword of Fire. Nya appeared in front of it.

"Nya!" Kai cried. He ran toward her.

"Don't worry, I'm right here," Nya said. But as she spoke, she transformed . . . into the dark shadow of Garmadon!

Garmadon moved aside, and Kai saw his real sister hanging above a pit of lava!

"In your world, I can't take the Sword of Fire," Garmadon said. "But you can take it for me."

Nya started to slide down toward the lava. Kai knew there was only one way to save her. He had to take the Sword and cut the chains.

Kai grabbed the Sword.
"Ninjago!" he cried.
He swirled and whirled, turning into a glowing, red tornado. Then he flew over the lava. He cut the chains and grabbed Nya. They landed safely on the rocks.

LORD GARMADON'S PLAN

Garmadon's shadow rose up in front of Kai. He swung the Sword, but it went right through the shadow! Then Garmadon kicked Kai, and Kai fell down.

"That's not fair!" cried Nya.

Garmadon's shadow made copies of itself. All the shadows attacked Kai. The Sword fell out of his hands.

Garmadon picked up the Sword. Then a new shadow jumped behind him. It was Sensei Wu!

The sensei used his own shadow to fight Garmadon's shadows. He got the Sword back.

"But what of the other three Weapons?" Lord Garmadon asked.

"They are safe!" Sensei Wu replied.

"Are you sure?" asked Garmadon.

Back at camp, a noise woke Cole. He gasped. Skeleton warriors Nuckal and Kruncha had captured Jay and Zane! Their king, Samukai, held the three Weapons of Spinjitzu in his bony hands.

"I believe these belong to Lord Garmadon now!" he said, grinning.

Back in the temple, Sensei Wu turned to Kai and Nya. "My brother must not unite the four Weapons," he warned them.

"Awaken, Guardian of the Sword!" Garmadon yelled. "Do not let them escape!"

A huge red dragon rose up from the bubbling lava. It spread its wings and roared.

A TRIP TO THE UNDERWORLD

There was only one escape — down into the Underworld.

Sensei Wu used the Sword to cut the rock beneath his feet. The rock floated on the lava, carrying him away.

"Sensei, no!" Kai cried.

"I must take the Sword of Fire to the Underworld," Sensei said firmly.

"I will see you there, brother," Garmadon
said, and his shadow disappeared.

"It's all my fault!" Kai wailed. "Sensei
won't be able to hold out for long."

"Forget Sensei," said Nya, looking up
at the angry dragon. "What about us?"

Back at camp, Samukai jumped into his Skull Truck. "To the Underworld!" he cried.

The skeleton warriors sped away, leaving Cole, Jay, and Zane behind.

"Now what?" Cole asked.

"Now we get out of here," Jay answered. He drew a sword he had taken from Nuckal. He cut the rope, and they all hit the ground.

The ninja raced after Samukai. They jumped onto the Skull Truck.

Smack! Pow! Cole went after Nuckal and Kruncha. Jay ran up and . . . *whack!* Cole accidentally hit him in the throat.

The Skull Truck reared up on its back wheels. Jay, Cole, and Zane tumbled off. The truck vanished into the Underworld.

Jay, Cole, and Zane ran to the red temple.

"I sense that the Weapons are in the Underworld," Zane said. "We are too late."

Then they heard Kai's voice. "We may not be able to cross over to the Underworld," he said, "but a dragon can."

The temple doors opened. The ninja gasped when they saw Kai and Nya riding the Fire Dragon!

DRAGON RIDERS

"Dragons belong to both worlds, so they can travel between them," Nya explained.

Cole shuddered. "No way!" He was terrified of dragons.

Kai jumped down and patted the dragon's head. "Once he realized we were trying to protect the Sword of Fire, he became quite a softie!"

Nya said good-bye to her brother. Soon the four ninja were flying across the sky, each one riding an elemental dragon.

"Easy, easy!" Cole said nervously, as the Earth Dragon soared across the sky.

"This is awesome!" Zane cried from the back of the Ice Dragon.

The dragons flew through the long, dark tunnel that led to the Underworld. They saw Garmadon's black palace in the distance. Skeleton warriors guarded the entrance.

"Sensei is inside," Zane said. "And they're expecting us."

To get past the warriors, the four ninja swung from the black rocks that hung down over the Underworld. Jay grabbed onto a long and skinny rock. He looked up — and saw that it was the leg of a giant spider!

"Brak, bleck, blah!" Jay cried, but his throat was still hurt. His friends didn't understand him.

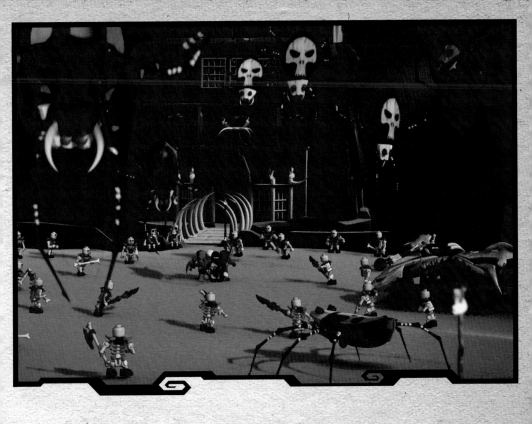

The other ninja finally looked up and saw
the spiders.

"*Aaaahhhh!*" they screamed. They let go and
fell to the ground. In an instant, the skeleton
warriors had surrounded them. Then the
spiders dropped down.

"Uh-oh!" Kai cried.

A BATTLE BETWEEN BROTHERS

Inside the palace, Sensei Wu heard a voice behind him.

"Brother," Garmadon said.

Sensei Wu spun around. He drew the Sword of Fire.

"Brother," he said.

"Seize the sword!" Garmadon yelled.

Skeleton warriors jumped out of the shadows. Sensei Wu used Spinjitzu. A golden tornado swirled around the room, knocking down the skeletons one by one.

"You'll have to take it from me!" Sensei Wu told his brother.

Samukai appeared. "My pleasure!" he growled, waving the other three Weapons of Spinjitzu. He let out a loud roar and charged at Sensei Wu.

The old man somersaulted right over Samukai's head. He swung the sword at Samukai, but the skeleton blocked it with the Scythe of Quakes.

TORNADO OF CREATION

Outside, the ninja needed a plan. Jay knew what to do.

"Brawr, blech, blah!" he cried.

"You need a vacation?" Kai asked.

Frustrated, Jay yelled as loud as he could. "Tornado of Creation!"

"Let's do this," said Cole. "Earth!"

"Fire!" yelled Kai.

"Ice!" cried Zane.

"Lightning!" shouted Jay.

"Ninjago!" yelled all four ninja. The four tornados burned brightly. Then they joined together. . . .

One giant, swirling tornado whipped through the palace courtyard. It picked up every warrior, spider, and object in its path. Then the tornado spat them out.

Now they were all transformed . . . into a giant Ferris wheel made of bones! The skeleton warriors were trapped inside.

"Come on! There's no time to waste!" Kai cried.

SHOWDOWN WITH LORD GARMADON

    The four ninja hurried into the palace.
They saw Sensei Wu battling Samukai.
    Sensei Wu fought hard, but it was one
Weapon against three. Samukai used the
Shurikens of Ice to freeze the Sword. Then
he used the Scythe of Quakes to shake the
ground. Finally, he hurled the Nunchuks of
Lightning at Sensei Wu, shocking him.
    The Sword fell out of Sensei Wu's hands.

"Bring me the four Weapons," Garmadon demanded.

Samukai picked up the Sword. "No! You will obey me now!" he told Garmadon.

The Weapons began to shake and glow. Garmadon laughed.

"No one can handle all that power at once," Sensei Wu said.

"What's happening to me?" Samukai
wailed.

"You have fallen into my master plan,"
Garmadon replied. "Not even I can handle
the power of all four Weapons. But now
that they have combined, it will create a
vortex through space and time. I can finally
escape the Underworld!"

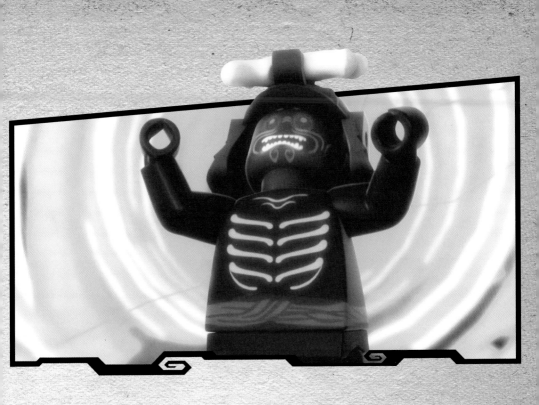

Boom! Samukai vanished in a storm of white light. A glowing blue tunnel appeared. Garmadon went toward it.

"Soon I will be strong enough to hold the four Weapons!" he boasted. "Then I will make the world in my image!"

The vortex disappeared — and so did Garmadon.

"He is gone," Sensei Wu said. "But he will return."

Kai picked up the Sword of Fire. Jay
picked up the Nunchuks. Cole grabbed
the Scythe, and Zane took the Shurikens.
"Then we'll be ready for him!" Kai vowed.

TRAINING DAY

"Let's do it! Hiii-yah!"

Sensei Wu heard the sound of ninja training echo through the dojo. But the training room was empty. Puzzled, Sensei Wu opened the door to the dojo's parlor.

Cole, Zane, Jay, and Kai weren't training. They were playing a ninja video game!

Sensei Wu unplugged the game.

"Just because Lord Garmadon escaped doesn't mean he won't return," Sensei Wu told them. "You must keep up with your training."

"We can train tomorrow," Cole said.

"Never put off until tomorrow what can be done today," Sensei Wu said.

Cole smiled. "Then I guess I'll eat this pizza today."

"No pizza!" Sensei Wu yelled. "In order to reach your full potential, you must train!"

"Don't worry, master," said Zane. "We'll be ready when Lord Garmadon returns."

Kai's sister, Nya, ran into the room.

"Guys! Lord Garmadon has returned!" she cried.

The ninja quickly grabbed the four Golden Weapons of Spinjitzu. Kai held the Sword of Fire. Cole held the Scythe of Quakes. Zane held the Shurikens of Ice. Jay held the Nunchuks of Lightning.

Then each ninja climbed onto his dragon, and they streaked through the sky to the village.

CRASH LANDING

The ninja were a little out of practice. They came to a crash landing in Jamanakai Village. The frightened villagers were screaming and running into their homes.

A tall, black shadow loomed over the village. Lord Garmadon!

Quickly, the ninja ran to face him. They drew their Weapons.

A figure in black stepped forward. But it wasn't Lord Garmadon, it was a little boy.

"It is I — Lloyd Garmadon!" he cried.

"He must be Lord Garmadon's son," Cole realized.

"Give me your candy, or I'll release the Serpentine on you!" Lloyd threatened. He opened a jar, and toy snakes sprang out.

"Does he really think he can scare people with an old bedtime story?" Kai asked.

"The Serpentine are real, Kai," Zane said seriously.

"Yeah, right," Kai said. "So, I'm supposed to believe an ancient race of snake people that used to rule Ninjago are now locked underground?"

The ninja didn't take Lloyd seriously. They
hung him by his pants from a sign in town.

"I will get my revenge on you all!" Lloyd
yelled.

The ninja just laughed. Zane bought some
candy, and they ate it in front of Lloyd.

"*Mmm*, cotton candy," Jay said, taking
a big bite.

THE PROPHECY

The ninja went back to their dragons. As Kai climbed aboard his, a scroll fell out of a bag attached to the saddle.

"That's Sensei's bag," Zane said. "You must have taken it by accident."

Zane read from the scroll. It revealed a prophecy about the future.

"One ninja will rise above the others and become the Green Ninja, the ninja destined to defeat the dark lord," Zane read.

"You think they mean Lord Garmadon?" Cole asked.

They looked at the scroll. Besides the green ninja, there were four other ninja: one red, one blue, one black, and one white.

"Wait a minute. Is that us?" Kai asked.

"Is anyone else thinking what I'm thinking?" Kai asked.

"Like how good I'm going to look in green?" Jay replied.

"Technically, *I* am the best," Zane pointed out.

Cole got angry. "Everyone, stop it! We're a team, remember? We weren't even supposed to see this scroll. Let's go back and train."

While the ninja flew back to the dojo, Lloyd
stomped through the snowy mountains.

"Stupid ninja! I'll show them!" he said, kicking
the rocks at his feet.

Clang! One of the rocks hit something hard.
Curious, Lloyd pushed away the snow. He
found a stone with strange carvings on it.

Lloyd pulled a lever, and the stone began
to slide open!

THE SERPENTINE

"Aaaaaah!"

Lloyd stumbled and fell through the hole down into an icy chamber. He stood up — and then he heard a creepy voice behind him.

"You are out of your mind to travel *sssso* far away from home, little one."

Lloyd gasped. A *real* Serpentine slithered toward him!

"Look into my *eyesss*," the snake creature hissed, and his eyes glowed red. "I will control your mind."

Terrified, Lloyd stepped backward. He ducked to avoid the Serpentine's hypnotizing eyes.

Lloyd had backed into a column of ice. The Serpentine saw his own reflection in the ice. He had hypnotized himself by mistake!

Lloyd grinned. "No. I will control *you* from now on!"

Lloyd didn't know it yet, but he had control of a Serpentine general, the leader of the Hypnobrai tribe.

"What will you have *usss* do, *massster*?" the general hissed.

As he spoke, the Hypnobrai soldiers marched out of the shadows.

"My own army of snakes!" Lloyd yelled. "*Mwahahahaha!*"

A LITTLE FRIENDLY COMPETITION

Back at the dojo, the four ninja decided to hold a tournament.

"Last one standing is the Green Ninja!" Kai exclaimed.

First Kai and Jay faced off. But neither ninja could control his Golden Weapon. Jay got a shock from his own Nunchuks. And Kai's Sword shot out energy blasts when he didn't expect it. But Kai still managed to win.

"Ninjago!" Kai cried, and Cole and Zane began to battle. At first, Cole couldn't control his Scythe. Zane tried to freeze him in place with the power of his Shurikens. But Cole knocked down Zane for the win.

Now it was Cole against Kai. Who would win?

But they never found out — because Kai's Sword set the training room on fire!

Sensei Wu arrived just in time. He used the Shurikens of Ice to put out the fire.

"What were you thinking?" he asked angrily.

"We want to know . . . which one of us is the chosen one?" Kai asked.

"None of you," Sensei Wu replied, "if you don't unlock your full potential! None of you are near the level of the Green Ninja."

NYA'S DISCOVERY

While Sensei scolded the boys, Nya was visiting Jamanakai Village. Suddenly, she heard villagers screaming.

Lloyd Garmadon marched through the town, followed by the Hypnobrai army. The general and Scales, his second-in-command, stood at his side.

"Take the candy! Take it all!" Lloyd yelled.

Nya quickly hid behind a building. She watched the general, who held a golden staff. His red eyes began to glow and spin. He hypnotized all the villagers.

Nya listened as Scales argued with the general.

"Why are we raiding a town just to get sweets?" Scales asked.

"You will do as I say, because I hold the staff!" the general replied.

Back at the dojo, Sensei Wu had a vision of the village. He ran to the training room.

"The Serpentine are back!" he told the ninja. "Everyone in Jamanakai Village is in danger!"

RESCUE MISSION

The ninja hurried to their dragons and flew back to the village. They found Lloyd pushing a wheelbarrow full of candy.

"Sorry, Little Garmadon, but it's past your bedtime!" Kai said.

Lloyd scowled. He turned to his army. "Get them!" he yelled.

"*Sssseize them!*" the general hissed.

The Hypnobrai army and the hypnotized villagers surrounded the four ninja. Jay twirled his Nunchuks, ready to fight.

"No! The Weapons are too unstable!" Zane warned.

"I guess that leaves us with . . . RUN!" Jay yelled.

The ninja ran into Nya.

"They've hypnotized everyone in town," she told them. "When you hear them rattle their tails, don't look them in the eyes!"

"How are we going to fight them with our eyes closed?" Jay asked.

"We need to get the staff from the general," Nya said. "It holds the antivenom. We can use it to break the spell on the villagers."

The ninja split up and raced off to find the general. Kai was quickly surrounded by Hypnobrai soldiers.

"Wanna play?" he asked them. "How about a little Spinjitzu? *Ninjaaaago!*"

Kai began to spin, becoming a twirling tornado of red energy. But he was so out of practice that he couldn't control his path. He slammed into a wall!

Zane saw Lloyd escaping with the candy. He threw his Shurikens in front of Lloyd, and they froze the ground in his path. Lloyd stopped short, and the candy tumbled out of his wheelbarrow.

"We should have dealt with you the first time," Zane said.

"Retreat!" Lloyd cried.

THE POWER OF THE SNAKES

The Serpentine army tried to flee the village. But Cole stopped the general with a high kick. The staff fell to the ground. Cole picked it up.

The general ran away, but Scales stood his ground. "Look into my *eyesssss*," he hissed. "I control you."

"Cole!" Nya cried. She ran between Cole and Scales. Then she jumped up and kicked the snake creature.

Scales hurried away. Nya pointed to the staff in Cole's hands.

"You have the antivenom!" she yelled. "Quick, the fountain!"

Cole jumped onto the big fountain in the center of the village. He placed the staff in the water, and a blue mist rose up. The villagers breathed it in. Soon they were back to normal.

Sensei Wu walked through the mist.

"We're sorry, Sensei," Kai told him. "If we had dealt with Lloyd before he became a problem, none of this would have happened."

"Even lessons learned the hard way are lessons learned," Sensei Wu replied kindly. Then he grew serious. "A great evil has been released. I fear troubling times are coming."

That trouble was brewing deep in the tomb of the Hypnobrai.

"I hold the key to destroying the ninja!" Scales bragged. His eyes glowed red.

Back in the dojo, Cole's eyes glowed red, too. Scales still controlled Cole . . . and when the time was ready, he would strike.

LEGO NINJAGO
Masters of Spinjitzu

A NINJA'S PATH

PREPARING FOR THE ENEMY

High in his mountain dojo, Sensei Wu was thinking about the Serpentine army. The snake creatures, led by Lloyd Garmadon, were a threat to Ninjago.

Luckily, Sensei Wu's ninja had taken the Serpentine general's staff. With the staff, the ninja could fight the effects of the Serpentine's hypnotic powers.

Up on the rooftop, Kai, Cole, Jay, and Zane were training. Each ninja had one of the Golden Weapons of Spinjitzu. Jay's Nunchuks spit out electric sparks. Kai's Sword blazed with fire. Cole swung his powerful Scythe.

Zane meditated quietly. Then he jumped up and began to spin. His Shurikens of Ice froze the whole rooftop!

"It's like Zane's in his own world," Jay complained.

"Sensei, Zane's weird," Kai told their teacher as he entered the room.

"What is weird?" Sensei asked. "Someone who is different, or someone who is different from *you*?"

"No, Sensei. He's *weird* weird," Cole insisted.

"Like when we watched that sad movie — and he laughed!" Jay said.

"Or the time he started grooming himself in the bathroom!" Cole complained. "Right in front of me! Like I wasn't even there!"

"We like the guy," Kai said. "He's really smart. He's just a little . . . off sometimes."

"Zane is a brother, and brothers are often different," Sensei Wu told him. His face darkened as he thought of his own brother, the evil Lord Garmadon. "I should know."

A gong rang out.

"Mail!" cried Kai, Jay, and Cole. They ran to get their letters and packages. But there was nothing for Zane.

"Hey, Zane . . . how come you don't ever hear from your parents?" Jay asked.

"I don't remember my parents," Zane replied. "I've been an orphan all my life."

A SERPENTINE SPY

Cole opened a package for his dragon, Rocky — a tasty toad. As he fed Rocky, someone was watching — through Cole's own eyes!

The watcher was a Serpentine named Scales. He had hypnotized Cole during a battle in Jamanakai Village. Now he could see everything Cole saw.

The Serpentine soldiers were busy building a tree house for Lloyd Garmadon. Scales thought it was a silly idea.

"I must question *thisss* childish agenda," he told the general. "The ninja have our staff. We should get it back."

"How dare you question me?" demanded the general.

Back at the dojo, it was Zane's turn to cook.

"Dinner is served!" he announced.

When the other ninja caught sight of him, they all laughed. Zane was wearing a frilly pink apron.

"What's so funny?" Zane asked. He didn't think it was strange at all.

"Well, how about this?" Cole asked. He mashed his plate of food in Kai's face. "Now *that's* funny!"

Then Sensei Wu dumped his food on top of Cole's head. A food fight started. Everyone laughed and joined in — except for Zane.

That night, Zane looked up at the stars.

Is this the place I really belong? he wondered.

A falcon landed on a tree branch near Zane. Zane shook his head, and the bird shook its head. Zane flapped his arms, and the bird flapped his wings. Who was this strange new friend?

Zane followed the falcon into the forest. The bird led him to the Serpentine's fort. Then it flew off into the night.

MISSION: TREE HOUSE

Zane ran and got his friends. The four ninja raced through the forest.

"So, tell us again how you found Lloyd's secret headquarters?" Kai asked.

"I followed a bird," Zane explained.

The ninja laughed — until they saw that Zane was right.

"It looks like those three trees are holding up the whole thing," Kai said. "Once we untie the ropes, the whole thing will fall."

The four ninja sneaked into the fort and spied on Lloyd.

"You! Hold up that sign for me!" Lloyd yelled at one of the snake soldiers.

The soldier held up a sign that read, "No Girls or Ninja."

The ninja split up. Jay raced to one of the ropes holding up the fort.

"Ninjago!" he yelled. Then he twirled, using Spinjitzu to cut through the rope.

"Ninjago!" Zane took down the second rope. The fort began to fall apart.

"I said NO ninja!" Lloyd yelled. "Attack!"

"Cole, wait until we're out of the fort. Then cut the last line!" Kai called.

Cole nodded. But Scales saw him.

"You are under my command," he hissed.

Scales ordered Cole to fight the other ninja. Then he raised his scaly fist in the air. "Now to get the staff!"

The tree house swayed back and forth. But the ninja couldn't jump off. They were too busy fighting Cole!

"Friends don't hit friends," Jay said.

But Cole attacked them with the Scythe of Quakes.

The others didn't want to hurt him. Jay used his Nunchuks of Lightning to try to shock Cole out of his trance.

Bam! The lightning hit Cole. Cole bounced back to his feet, angry. He pushed Jay off the tree house.

Then Cole ran to the last rope and raised his Scythe. Once he cut the rope, the tree house — and all the ninja — would fall.

"No, Cole!" Jay, Kai, and Zane cried.

Suddenly, the sound of a flute filled the air. Cole put down the Scythe.

It was Sensei Wu! He and Nya flew to the rescue on Kai's dragon.

"That flute cancels their powers!" Jay realized.

"Where am I?" Cole asked. "What are we doing?"

"We're getting out of here because this whole place is coming down!" Nya warned.

The four ninja jumped onto the dragon. *Boom!* The tree house crashed to the ground.

"We must hurry!" Sensei Wu said. "The dojo is unguarded!"

RAIDED!

But they were too late. The dojo was in flames!

Kai made a fist. "Those snakes!"

The dragons were trapped in the burning stable. Cole quickly pulled a lever and set them free.

Zane called to his dragon. "Shard! Put this out!"

Shard blasted the flames with his icy breath. The fire went out, but it was too late.

Kai looked around at the ruins. "Our home," he said sadly. "It's all gone."

Kai, Jay, and Cole were angry with Zane.

"If you hadn't followed that silly bird, none of this would have happened!" Kai yelled.

"Enough!" Sensei Wu cried. "Zane is your brother. Say you are sorry."

But when the boys turned around, Zane was gone.

THE SLITHER PIT

The Serpentine stole the staff from the dojo. Then they went back to their icy underground tomb. Scales proudly held the staff.

"Give me back my staff!" the general demanded.

"No," Scales said. "We will have to fight for it — in the Slither Pit!"

A soldier took the staff from Scales. "Winner gets the staff and leads the tribe!" he yelled. "There are no rules. Now fight!"

Weapons made of ice lowered from the ceiling. The general grabbed a shield and an axe. Scales grabbed two swords.

"Go, General!" Lloyd yelled.

The general whipped his long tail at Scales. But Scales used fang-kwon-do.

"Hii-yaaah!" He kicked the general in the chin, and the general fell back. He couldn't get up. Scales had won!

A soldier handed the staff to Scales. His feet began to glow. They turned into a long blue tail. Scales was the general now!

"Scales! Scales! Scales!" the Serpentine shouted.

The old general's tail turned into legs.

"You will be loyal to *me* now!" Scales told him. Then he turned to Lloyd. "Leave and never return!"

The snakes left Lloyd outside in the frozen wilderness. But before he left, he stole their map.

Back at the mountain, Cole, Jay, Kai, Nya, and Sensei Wu huddled around a fire. They were cold and tired — and eating mud newt for dinner.

"We must be thankful for what we still have," Sensei Wu reminded them.

"What do we have?" Cole asked. "We don't have our home."

"I don't miss our home," Kai said. "I miss Zane."

Just then, Zane came walking up the mountain.

"Zane, we're so sorry for everything we said!" Jay said.

"Why?" Zane asked. "That is not why I left. I saw the falcon again. Come, let me show you what I have found."

"I feel a strange connection with that falcon," Zane explained as they walked. "I think he is trying to show us the path we need to take."

They walked over a hill, and then they saw it — a deserted ship. It looked warm and cozy.

"Do I smell pie?" Jay asked.

Zane smiled. "Yes. I made dinner."

The ninja let out a cheer and ran to the ship.

"Thank you, Zane," Sensei Wu said. "One day, we will find your family."

"I've already found them," Zane replied. He smiled and looked at his friends.

NINJAGO
Masters of Spinjitzu

PIRATES VS. NINJA

PATIENCE, LLOYD!

"*Hii-yah!* Fists of Fury!" Lloyd yelled, pounding his fist into Kai's palm.

Ninja Cole, Jay, Kai, and Zane were training Lloyd in their Ninjago City apartment. It had been their home since evil Lord Garmadon had stolen the *Destiny's Bounty*, their flying ship. But a kitchen was no place to train a ninja. Kai had to use oven mitts for gloves.

"Lloyd, you are late for your next lesson with Nya," said Sensei Wu.

"*Aw!* But when will I learn Spinjitzu?" Lloyd whined.

"Patience," Sensei Wu told him. "Your Spinjitzu will only be unlocked when the key is ready to be found."

Sighing, Lloyd went off to see Kai's sister, Nya, a samurai warrior.

Lloyd found Nya stroking the nose of a four-headed dragon. The great beast was sick.

"One day, he'll be yours," Nya said. "Ultra Dragon is meant for the Green Ninja to ride."

The dragon's four heads roared.

"Looks like he's feeling better," Lloyd said as the dragon flew off.

Lloyd was destined to become the legendary Green Ninja. Sensei Wu sent the ninja to find a better place to train him.

"These will transport you any place you want to go," Sensei said with a smile. "They are bus tokens!"

THE MEGA WEAPON'S POWER

    Meanwhile, Lord Garmadon and his crew of Serpentine warriors flew high above Ninjago City aboard the *Destiny's Bounty*, the ancient pirate ship Garmadon had stolen from the ninja. He also had their magical Weapons. Combined, they formed the Mega Weapon.

    Lord Garmadon only had one problem. He didn't know how the Weapon worked!

"We spotted something!" one of the crew members cried. He pointed to Ultra Dragon as it flew past the ship.

"Don't let him get away, you slithering idiots!" Garmadon yelled. He pointed the Weapon at the dragon. "Destroy!"

But the Weapon didn't do anything.

Garmadon stormed belowdecks. He pounded the Weapon on a table.

A secret door opened, and an old journal popped out. Lord Garmadon read the story of Captain Soto. The pirate and his crew had sailed the ship two hundred years before.

"This crew sounds like they knew how to handle a ship," Garmadon said. "I wish they were here to show these scaly idiots how it's done!"

Suddenly, the Mega Weapon began to sizzle and smoke.

"What is happening?" Lord Garmadon wailed. "It won't let me let go!"

Then he heard a voice overhead. "All hands on deck! I am Captain Soto!"

PIRATES ON BOARD

Lord Garmadon rushed to the deck. Captain Soto and his pirate crew had come to life! They waved their swords at the snakes.

"I asked for a better crew, and I got it," Lord Garmadon realized. "The Mega Weapon has the power to create!" But using it had left him very weak.

Captain Soto marched up to Lord Garmadon. "I be Captain Soto, Stealer of the Seas!" the pirate snarled. "We are taking back our ship."

Then he turned to his crew. "Lock him and all his reptilian friends in the brig!"

Lord Garmadon was too weak to fight back. The pirates locked him and the Serpentine warriors in the ship's jail.

On deck, Captain Soto discovered that his ship could fly.

"This is too good!" He chuckled as they flew toward Ninjago City. "Just wait till they get a load of us!"

FOLLOW THAT SHIP!

Back in the city, the ninja had found a new place to train: Grand Sensei Dareth's Mojo Dojo. But Dareth was no Sensei Wu.

"I am a karate machine," Dareth bragged. But when he tried to show off his skills, he just got tangled up.

The ninja got busy training Lloyd. Cole showed Lloyd how to break a stack of boards.

Bam! Lloyd broke the boards — and the floor, too!

"With this power, you must be careful," Sensei Wu warned. "You must control it before it controls you."

Then the ninja heard screams outside. The pirates were attacking the city!

"You must stay here," Zane told Lloyd. "Your powers are not ready yet."

A bus pulled up, and the ninja hopped on.

"Follow that ship!" Kai told the driver.

DARETH WALKS THE PLANK

Grand Sensei Dareth wanted to impress the ninja. He jumped onto the pirate ship from a rooftop.

"Surrender, or face the brown ninja!" he cried.

"Pajama Man! Get him!" yelled Captain Soto.

Dareth's silly karate moves were no match for the pirates. They grabbed him and tied him up.

"Keep an eye out for any other masked Pajama People," Captain Soto told his crew.

Back in Ninjago City, Cole, Jay, Kai, and Zane knew that they needed disguises. They put on pirate costumes and sneaked onboard the floating ship.

Captain Soto was making Dareth walk the plank!

The ninja couldn't save Dareth. Captain Soto pushed him off the plank!

"*Aaaaah!*" Dareth screamed as he fell.

"*Yee-hah!*" Lloyd appeared, riding the Ultra Dragon! He swooped down from the sky. The dragon caught Dareth in one of its mouths.

WHO WILL WIN?

"Ninjago!" the four ninja yelled. They used Spinjitzu to transform into their ninja outfits.

Captain Soto looked confused. "More Pajama Men?"

"Ninja versus pirates," Kai said. "Who will win?"

Cole jumped across the deck. He used his scythe to slice the feather off Captain Soto's hat.

The battle had begun!

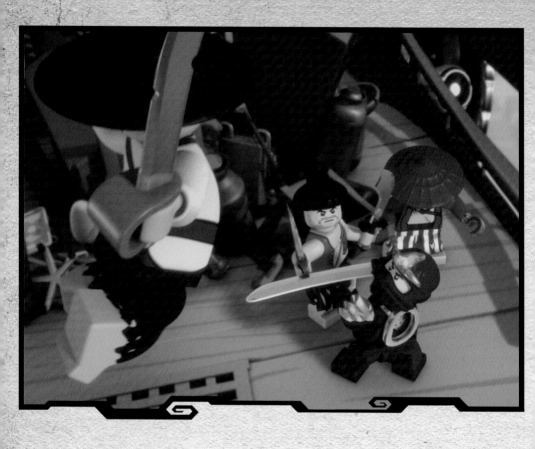

Three pirates surrounded Kai. He thrust his sword into the deck.

Whap! Whap! Whap! He grabbed the hilt and swung around, kicking the pirates away.

Another pirate charged at Zane. He held a sharp dagger in each hand.

Crack! Zane used his whip to send the pirate flying backward.

Kai and Cole fought off two pirates. Jay had an idea. He used his nunchuks to break open a gumball machine.

The gumballs spilled out onto the deck. *Splat!* The pirates tripped and fell down — and so did Kai and Cole.

"Oops!" Jay said.

A BARREL OF TROUBLE

"Ninjago!" Lloyd yelled. He jumped off the Ultra Dragon and landed on the pirate ship.

Captain Soto charged at Lloyd. Kai jumped between them.

"Lloyd! You're not supposed to be here!" Kai yelled. He stuffed Lloyd in a wooden barrel to keep him safe.

With the barrel over his head, Lloyd couldn't see where he was going. He accidentally bumped into the lever that dropped the ship's anchor.

Then he bumped into Kai. Kai jumped on top of the barrel, and they rolled across the deck together.

Kai fell off the barrel . . . and fell off the ship!

"*Whoa!*" he screamed.

He grabbed on to the anchor dangling from the ship. He clung to it as the anchor tore up the streets of Ninjago City.

A SURPRISE RESCUE

Back on the *Destiny's Bounty*, Captain Soto attacked Lloyd's barrel.

"Ninjago!" Lloyd cried.

He began to spin, turning into a green tornado of energy. The barrel exploded into pieces.

"I just did Spinjitzu for the first time!" Lloyd cheered.

Down below, Kai and the anchor were about to slam into a gas truck. If they hit it, the explosion would rock Ninjago City.

Up on the ship . . . *bam!* Captain Soto hit Lloyd from behind.

Lloyd fell into the lever that worked the anchor. It pulled the anchor back up to the ship — just in time!

Lloyd powered up with Spinjitzu — but he couldn't control his new abilities. Sizzling green light knocked down the mast of the ship. It crashed onto the ninja, trapping them all.

"You lose, Pajama People," Captain Soto said with an evil grin. "Now you're walking the plank."

Boom! Boom! Boom! The ship began to shake. The pirates looked up, and saw a giant robot stomping toward them.

It was Nya, piloting her giant samurai robot! She picked up the big mast and knocked down the pirate crew. Then she jumped out, slid down the ship's sails, and landed on Captain Soto.

"Who wins between pirates and ninja?" Jay asked. "It's samurai!"

The Ninjago City police rounded up the pirates. "That your ship?" an officer asked the ninja.

Lord Garmadon was flying away on the *Destiny's Bounty*. "You snooze, you lose!"

"Great," Jay sighed. "Lord Garmadon's back, and now he's got our ship?"

Cole mussed Lloyd's hair. "Well, at least we've got this little guy!"

Lloyd grinned. He couldn't wait until he could be the Green Ninja all the time!

NINJAGO
Masters of Spinjitzu

THE GREEN NINJA

KID STUFF

"We've been training all day," Lloyd complained to his four ninja friends, Cole, Jay, Kai, and Zane.

"We have to get you ready to face your father," Cole reminded him. Lloyd was the Green Ninja — the only one who could take down the evil Lord Garmadon.

"But the latest edition of *Starfarer* just came in to Doomsday Comics," Lloyd said.

"Sorry, Lloyd," Kai said, "but as the Green Ninja, you don't have time for kid stuff."

Nya ran onto the deck of *Destiny's Bounty*, the ninja's flying ship. "Guys! Lord Garmadon has broken into the Ninjago Museum of Natural History."

"Let me guess," Lloyd said. "This mission is too dangerous for me, right?"

"Right!" the four ninja agreed.

Inside the museum, Lord Garmadon held the Mega Weapon. It was a magical Weapon with the power to create.

"Behold . . . the Grundle!" Lord Garmadon cried. He pointed to a skeleton of a huge, fierce-looking beast. "It is now extinct. But when it roamed Ninjago, it could track any ninja."

RISE OF THE GRUNDLE

Lord Garmadon pointed the Mega Weapon at the Grundle skeleton.

"Rise, Grundle!" he commanded.

The Weapon sizzled with blue sparks. Purple energy waves flowed over the skeleton.

The four ninja burst into the museum. Garmadon's Serpentine warriors tried to stop them.

But the ninja were fast. They jumped on top of the Grundle. The snake warriors charged them. They knocked Cole, Jay, and Zane off the Grundle's back.

Kai threw his sword at Lord Garmadon, knocking the Mega Weapon from his hand. The purple energy faded.

"Not again!" Lord Garmadon wailed.

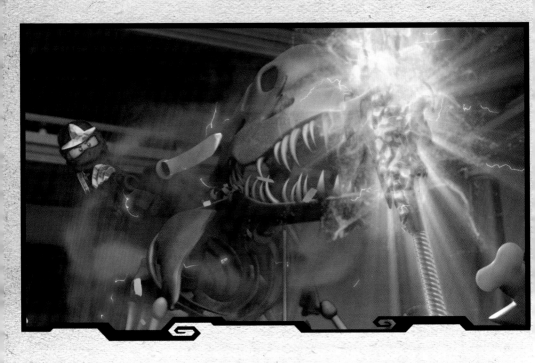

"*Ha-ha!* We stopped him! It didn't work!" Jay cheered.

Lord Garmadon ran off. His snake warriors followed him, carrying a golden sarcophagus along with them.

"They're stealing it!" Kai cried. "After them!"

The ninja raced out of the museum and onto the street. The sarcophagus was heavy, so the snakes dropped it and escaped.

THE INCREDIBLE SHRINKING NINJA

"I don't remember that sarcophagus being so big," Kai remarked.

"Did it grow?" Jay asked.

"Or did we shrink?" wondered Zane.

Suddenly, Kai noticed their reflection in a store window. "Uh, guys?"

"We *shruuuunk*!" Jay screamed.

It was worse than that. The ninja had been turned back into kids!

"I hate being a kid!" Cole wailed. "You can't drive. Nobody listens to you. Oh, no . . . bedtimes!"

"Garmadon must have made us younger with the Mega Weapon," Zane guessed.

At that moment, a police car screeched to a stop next to them.

"Looks like we caught the museum thieves!" the police officer said.

The ninja tried to explain what had really happened, but the police didn't believe them. Cole, Jay, Kai, and Zane spent the night in the police station.

Back at the ship, Nya and Sensei Wu were worried about them.

"Lloyd, you're in charge of the *Bounty* while Nya and I have a look around town," Sensei Wu told him.

ONE ANCIENT MONSTER

The next morning, the police brought the ninja and the sarcophagus back to the museum.

"Thank you," said the director. "But what about the Grundle?" He pointed to an empty display case.

"You don't think it just walked out of here?" Jay wondered.

"It is possible that Garmadon made the Grundle younger, too," Zane said, "and brought it back to life!"

Jay ran up to the grownups. "You guys have to believe us! The Grundle has been brought back to life, and it's on the loose!"

The director and the police just laughed.

"You boys wait here until we call your parents to pick you up," an officer told them.

"We gotta get out of here — like, now!" Cole warned the other ninja.

The ninja pretended to be part of a school group. They sneaked out of the museum.

"This is so humiliating!" Jay wailed.

"We can't use Spinjitzu in these bodies," Zane pointed out. "We are no match for the Grundle."

"Then we have to get back to the *Bounty*!" Kai told his friends.

THE GRUNDLE RETURNS

Rawr! As the ninja hurried away, a loud roar came from the museum. A huge, red beast with sharp claws and teeth jumped off the roof.

It was the Grundle! The great beast hated the sunlight. It stomped off to find a place to sleep until the sun went down. The people of Ninjago screamed and ran when they saw it.

The ninja didn't see the Grundle. They found a pay phone and called the *Destiny's Bounty*.

Lloyd answered the phone. "Where are you?" he asked. "Sensei is out looking for you."

"We can't explain now," Jay said. "Just meet us at Buddy's Pizza in ten minutes — and bring our weapons."

Ten minutes later, Lloyd strolled into the pizza parlor.

"*Pssst!* Lloyd!" Kai whispered.

"Beat it, brat! I'm on a mission," Lloyd said. He thought Kai was just some kid.

"It's me, Kai!" Kai told him.

Lloyd gasped. "Whoa! What happened? You're ... . small!"

Cole, Jay, Kai, and Zane explained how Lord Garmadon had brought the Grundle to life — and turned them into kids at the same time.

"We can't defeat the Grundle until we're back to full strength," Kai said. "We need to find someone who knows how to fight that thing."

Lloyd grinned. "I think I know just the guy!"

COMIC-BOOK HEROES

Lloyd brought the ninja to a comics shop.

"We're not gonna pick up your stupid comic, Lloyd," Kai complained. "This is serious business!"

Suddenly, Jay let out a happy cry. "Look! A new issue of Daffy Dale!"

"Boys, this is Rufus McAllister, also known as Mother Doomsday," Lloyd said. "He owns this place."

"Rufus, what do you know about the Grundle?" Lloyd asked.

"I know all about that extinct beast," Rufus said. "One, its thick hide can't be hurt by any weapons. Two, it only hunts at night. And three, the only way to defeat it is with light."

The ninja nervously looked out the window. The sun was going down fast.

"The Illuma Sword is the best weapon for fighting a Grundle," Rufus said. "That is, if you can get close enough to use it."

"We'll take the light swords," Kai said eagerly.

"Not so fast," said Rufus. "You'll have to win these swords in a *Starfarer* trivia battle."

"Sign me up!" Lloyd said.

Before the contest started, Lloyd got a
message to Sensei Wu.

"There is only one person who can turn the
ninja back to normal," Sensei Wu told Nya. They
hurried to Mystake's tea shop and explained
their problem.

"You need Tomorrow's Tea," the old woman
told them. "I should have one here somewhere."

Back at the comic shop, the contest began. Lloyd and two other kids answered questions about the *Starfarer* comic book and its hero, Fritz Donegan. It came down to Lloyd and just one other player.

"Lloyd! Lloyd! Lloyd!" the ninja cheered.

"Here's your final question," Rufus said. "In the latest issue, how does Fritz Donegan escape the Imperial Sludge?"

"B-b-but I didn't read the latest issue," Lloyd stammered.

Just then, the lights in the comic shop flickered. The whole room began to shake.

"It's here," Kai whispered.

ATTACK OF THE GRUNDLE

"What's here?" Rufus asked nervously.

They all looked up at the glass roof. A huge, scary figure loomed above them.

Crunch! A huge, scaly foot stomped down, smashing the glass.

Everyone screamed and ran.

Crash! The Grundle fell through the ceiling. The ninja quickly ran and pulled on ninja outfits on display in the store. They each grabbed an Illuma Sword and charged the Grundle.

Hii-yaah! One by one, they attacked the Grundle, but the monster swatted them away like flies.

The Grundle hovered over them, its huge jaw open. Green slime dripped from its mouth.

"*Aaaaah!*" the ninja screamed.

"I'll take care of this," Lloyd said. He created a ball of energy in his hands and hurled it at the Grundle.

Swat! The Grundle knocked down Lloyd with its tail.

Suddenly, Nya and Sensei Wu burst through the door.

Sensei Wu held up a jar of glowing liquid. "Use this! It will turn time forward. You will grow up and the Grundle will turn back into a pile of bones."

He tossed the jar to Jay.

"Wait!" Cole cried. "What will happen to Lloyd? He'll grow old, too."

"Just do it!" Lloyd cried.

"We can't take away your childhood," Jay said. "It's not fair."

The Grundle charged at the ninja, and they fell backward. The jar flew out of Jay's hands and landed in Lloyd's lap.

Lloyd stood up. He threw the jar at the Grundle. It hit him in the nose, and a purple mist floated out.

THE GREEN NINJA

Purple light swirled, and the Grundle whirled around as the magic tea took effect. Then the great beast quickly crumbled into a pile of bones.

When the dust cleared, Kai, Jay, Cole, and Zane stood up. They were taller — and older.

"We're not kids anymore," Cole realized.

Lloyd slowly got to his feet. He was taller. His hair was thicker. His voice was deeper.

"I'm . . . older," he said slowly.

"The time for the Green Ninja to face his destiny has grown nearer," said Sensei Wu.

Lloyd looked at his friends. "I'm ready," he said confidently.

Lloyd's mind was racing. Now that he was older, he would be able to control his Spinjitzu better. But did he really have what it took to become the legendary Green Ninja?

Sensei Wu seemed to read his mind. "The time until the final battle has become shorter," he said. "But the Green Ninja has grown stronger!"

Dear Family and Friends of New Readers,

Welcome to Scholastic Reader. We have taken over ninety years' worth of experience with teachers, parents, and children and put it into a program that is designed to match your child's interest and skills. Each Scholastic Reader is designed to support your child's efforts to learn how to read at every age and every stage.

- First Reader
- Preschool – Kindergarten
- ABC's
- First words

- Beginning Reader
- Preschool – Grade 1
- Sight words
- Words to sound out
- Simple sentences

- Developing Reader
- Grades 1 – 2
- New vocabulary
- Longer sentences

- Growing Reader
- Grades 1 – 3
- Reading for inspiration and information

For ideas about sharing books with your new reader, please visit www.scholastic.com. Enjoy helping your child learn to read and love to read!

Happy Reading!

—Francie Alexander
Chief Academic Officer
Scholastic Inc.